SHERMY & SHAKE,

THE NOT-SO-NICE NEIGHBOR

SHERMY & SHAKE,

THE NOT-SO-NICE NEIGHBOR

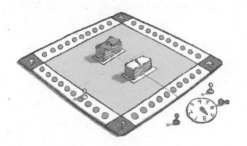

KIRBY LARSON

ILLUSTRATED BY
SHINJI FUJIOKA

CANDLEWICK PRESS

Text copyright © 2023 by Kirby Larson
Illustrations copyright © 2023 by Shinji Fujioka

First edition 2023

Library of Congress Catalog Card Number 2022908690
ISBN 978-1-5362-1942-5

23 24 25 26 27 28 LBM 10 9 8 7 6 5 4 3 2 1

Printed in Melrose Park, IL, USA

This book was typeset in Scala.
The illustrations were created digitally, late at night,
fueled by an unhealthy amount of caffeine.

Candlewick Press
99 Dover Street
Somerville, Massachusetts 02144

www.candlewick.com

For Clio and the Real Grandpa Gordy
KL

To pck, hehe . . .
SF

CONTENTS

...

JUNE

JULY

AUGUST

JUNE

GREETINGS, EARTHLING

■■■■

Shermy scooped up the last of the Sweetie Flakes from his cereal bowl. This was the best bite of all—just milk and sugar sludge. He smacked his lips.

"Mom, make him stop that!" His big sister, Brynn, peeked over her coding book.

Shermy slurped again. Extra loud.

Brynn covered her ears. "MO-om!"

"Shermy, mind your manners, please." Mom sipped her coffee. Quietly. "And don't forget to take out the trash."

Shermy squinted at the chore chart. He was sure it was Brynn's turn. But even without his glasses, he could see the magnet by his name. He picked up his bowl and drank the last of the milk. Then—CLANK—he dropped his spoon into the bowl.

Brynn jumped up from the table. "I'm going over to Kelsey's where I can concentrate."

"It's not me," Shermy said. "It's the cereal that's noisy."

"Brothers!" Brynn stomped out of the house, taking her book with her.

"Maybe I should start serving oatmeal," Mom said.

Shermy groaned. Dad was the oatmeal chef, not Mom. His was smooth and slid right down. Hers had lumps. Not even ten scoops of brown sugar could help him swallow it.

Shermy tiptoed to the dishwasher and carefully put

his bowl inside. "I promise to chew quiet as a mouse the whole summer."

"Thank you." Mom took a good look at him. "A vacation from school does not mean a vacation from wearing your glasses." She wagged her finger. "Go put them on."

"You said to take out the trash!" Shermy grabbed the trash bag with one hand and pinched his nose shut with the other. He zoomed outside to the garbage can, holding his breath while he lifted the lid. *Clunk.* In went the bag. *Thunk.* Down went the lid. He made it! Not one whiff of garbage air. Shermy did a little dance. This was his lucky day.

"Gree-tings, Earth-ling."

Shermy spun around at the sound of the robot voice. "Wh-what? Who said that?"

"It is I, Earth-ling. Greetings."

Without his glasses, Shermy could only see things that were close by. "Where are you?" he asked.

"Here!"

Rustle-crackle-rustle. The branches of Mrs. Brown's apple tree did a little dance.

"You're a tree?" Shermy asked.

"*In* the tree," the voice answered.

Shermy looked around for protection. There was only the garbage can lid. He yanked it up, held his breath, and took one step toward the fence. He couldn't see anyone . . . or any*thing.* "Who *are* you?"

"I am Falzar, from Jupiter," the voice answered.

"Are you . . . friendly?" Shermy asked. In the books he read, things didn't go well for humans if the aliens weren't friendly.

"When I'm not hungry," Falzar replied.

Shermy held the lid up higher and took a step back. "Are you . . . hungry?"

"I have come a long way, and my superpowers are running low," Falzar answered. "A Toaster Tart would taste very good."

"Toaster Tart?" said Shermy.

"Blueberry," said Falzar.

"How do you know about those?" Shermy asked.

"I've been studying Earthlings for a long time."

This sounded fishy. Shermy had never heard of aliens eating Earth food. "Show yourself," he said. "Or no Toaster Tart."

Rustle-crackle-rustle.

Shermy caught a glimpse of something shiny and silver.

Thump! Falzar jumped out of the tree. He brushed himself off and wiggled out of his space helmet.

"You're not from Jupiter!" Shermy set down the garbage can lid.

"You're right," said Falzar. "I'm from Walla Walla."

"Is that a real place?" This kid had already tried to trick Shermy once. Maybe he was doing it again.

"It sure is. And the people who founded it liked it so much they named it twice." The boy tossed the helmet in the air. "That's my stepdad's favorite joke."

"And you're not Falzar." Shermy should've figured it out sooner, seeing whose backyard the kid was in. "You're Mrs. Brown's grandson, Shake. She told me you were coming." Well, actually, Mrs. Brown hadn't told *Shermy*. She had told his mom when she came over for coffee. Shermy had been hanging around in case Mrs. Brown brought chocolate chip muffins again. But she hadn't brought anything except the news about Shake.

Shake's mom and stepfather were going on their honeymoon trip for the whole summer, so Shake was staying with his grandma. Shermy wasn't sure what a honeymoon trip was, but he guessed that kids weren't allowed.

"I knew you weren't from Jupiter." Shermy shoved his hands in his pockets. That would've been too much to hope for, even on the first day of summer vacation.

"But I would still like a Toaster Tart," said Shake. "Do you have any?"

"Maybe." Shermy pointed to Shake's helmet. "Can I wear that?"

"I'll think about it," Shake said. "After the Toaster Tart."

The boys went inside. Shermy climbed on a chair to get the last box of Toaster Tarts out of the cupboard. There were only two left inside.

"I may not be from Jupiter, but I do have superpowers." Shake snatched both Toaster Tarts and shoved them in his mouth. Without the toasting part!

"No fair!" Shermy's mouth watered.

"I told you I had superpowers," mumbled Shake.

Crumbs sprayed everywhere. "See how I made those disappear?"

Shermy tossed the empty box in the recycling. If he could make things disappear, he knew just where he'd start.

With Shake.

PUZZLES AND ICE POPS

■■■■

Shermy opened the jigsaw puzzle Grandpa Gordy had sent. It was a picture of the Grand Canyon. Going there was on their "Someday List." That meant they were for sure going to go there. Someday.

Shermy dumped the puzzle pieces onto the craft table and swirled them around. Grandpa Gordy taught him to sort out all the border pieces first. He held one up to see if it had a straight edge. Squinted. Yes. A border.

"That might be easier with your glasses," Mom said.

"Hmm." Shermy dumped a handful of middle pieces back in the box.

"Don't you remember that Dr. Margo said you need to wear them every day?" Mom tapped her paintbrushes against the sink and began to dry them with a towel.

"Okay, okay." After Shermy put his glasses on, he found two pieces that were already stuck together. Grandpa Gordy called that a "gimme."

There was a knock at the front door. Mom set her brushes down and went to answer it.

Shake raced into the kitchen. He pulled up a chair to the craft table. "Your mom called and told me to come over."

Shermy squinched his eyes at Mom. Had she forgotten about the other day? Shake had promised to be careful with Shermy's favorite Frisbee, and now it was stuck up on Mr. Wither's roof. Maybe if she was going to keep inviting Shake, she should play with him.

"I've been there." Shake pointed to the picture on the front of the puzzle box. "Mom and I camped in a tent. But we ate dinner in a fancy lodge." He grabbed a puzzle piece. "Sky," he said.

"Put it there." Shermy pointed to the bottom of the box. Middle pieces were like Someday Lists. You didn't do them right away. But you did do them. He and Grandpa would go to the Grand Canyon. They would sleep in a tent. And they would cook their dinner over a campfire.

Shake stretched across the table to reach the box. He bumped Shermy's border pile and pieces cascaded to the floor.

"Watch it." Shermy slid off his chair to pick up the pieces.

Shake didn't help one bit. "It's a nice day out," he said.

Shermy picked the last piece up off the floor. Tree.

"It's supposed to rain later on," Mom said. "That will be the perfect time for puzzles. Now is the perfect time for going outside." She latched her paint box.

"That's a neat wooden suitcase," Shake said.

"It's for my watercolors." Mom opened the box to show him.

"She got a blue ribbon on her painting," Shermy bragged. "The one of the peony."

"What's a peony?" Shake asked.

"A big red flower that smells good," Shermy said. "They probably don't have them in Walla Walla."

"Hear that?" Mom held her hand up to her ear. "The great outdoors is calling you boys."

"After I finish sorting." Shermy squinted at another puzzle piece. Not border.

Shake hopped up and jingled some change in his pocket. "Gram gave me money for the ice cream truck."

"I didn't hear the music." But Shermy stopped sorting.

"We saw it when we were coming back from the grocery store. Gram said it should be in our neighborhood soon." Shake jingled the change again. "I have money for you, too."

Shermy dropped the pieces he was holding. Mom was right. Puzzles were good for rainy afternoons. He followed Shake outside. Sure enough, he heard the ice cream truck bell. It wasn't very loud. Probably still a few blocks away.

His neighbors Clair and Esme were taking turns with a magnifying glass, studying a pill bug on Clair's front walk. "Are you waiting for the ice cream truck?" Clair asked.

Shake nodded and jingled his pocket again. "I have money for both of us."

"Are you Shermy's cousin or something?" Esme asked.

"No!" Shermy answered quickly. "This is Shake. Mrs. Brown's grandson."

"Can I take a look?" Shake asked.

Clair handed him the magnifying glass. "Be careful."

"I will," Shake said.

Shermy held his breath. That's what he'd said about the Frisbee.

"Do your eyes hurt?" Esme peered at Shermy. "They're scrunched up kind of funny."

"I just forgot to wear my glasses," Shermy said. He unscrunched his eyes after Shake handed back the magnifying glass in one piece.

"Listen!" Shake spun around. "It's getting louder!"

Ryan and Audrey, the twin sisters across the alley, came running outside. "I scream, you scream, we all scream for ice cream!" they sang.

"What are you going to get, Shermy?" Clair asked.

"In Walla Walla, everyone gets ice pops," said Shake.

Ice pops? When there were ice cream sandwiches and chocolate crunch bars and Sherbet Surprises? "Not me," said Shermy.

"I like ice pops," said Audrey.

"Me too," said Ryan. They always did everything the same.

"I hear the music! Here it comes!" cried Esme. The rest of the kids crowded in front of Shermy. A bunch of big kids pushed their way in, too.

The truck pulled over to the curb. The big kids bought all the ice creams. Even the ones with butterscotch.

"Guess we're getting ice pops," said Clair. But she didn't sound sad. "Which flavor's your favorite, Shake?"

"The rocket ones." Shake pointed at the skinny white-and-blue-with-red-on-top ice pops.

The girls giggled. They all picked rocket ice pops, then ran off to eat them.

By the time Shermy got to the truck, there was one rocket pop left.

"Dibs!" Shake snagged it.

The driver pulled out the last ice pop from the bottom of the freezer. Banana.

Shake paid for their treats. "Thanks," he said to the ice cream truck driver.

Shermy said thanks, too, even though he didn't feel very thankful for a banana ice pop. He walked back to his front porch. Shake followed him. They ate their treats.

Shake licked the wooden stick clean. "This is the best part." He stuck his tongue out. "Cool, huh?"

Right down the middle of his tongue was a cherry-red stripe. Like the kind on fancy race cars.

Mrs. Brown called Shake's name. "I better go." He jumped off the porch in one big leap and ran next door.

Shermy went inside to the bathroom and closed the door. He stood in front of the mirror and stuck out his tongue.

Plain old pink.

KING OF THE MOUNTAIN

■■■■

Shermy lay on the floor in his bedroom and turned another page in his library book. Mrs. Brown had taken Shake to the Imaginarium Museum. That meant Shermy could spend the whole day reading the latest Wilderness Adventures story. Happy as a puppy, he rolled from his back to his stomach as he started the next chapter. Reading slowly let him taste every word.

His bedroom door swung open. "Stay out, Brynn!" Shermy grumbled.

But it was Shake. He walked right in!

"Are you back already?" Shermy asked. He'd only made it to chapter three.

"Yeah. Gram got a headache. From getting wet." Shake picked up Shermy's glasses. Right off Shermy's own dresser. "Whoa! These make me dizzy." He reeled around the room.

Shermy got his glasses back and put them on. "How did she get wet?" he asked. It wasn't raining.

"Well, the first thing we did when we got there was play truck driver. I honked the horn about fifty times, then Gram said it was someone else's turn. After that, we did a science experiment where I rubbed a balloon on her hair to make it stand up by itself. Then we went to the outside play area and there was this cool water cannon. The water came out really fast and I let go of the hose and accidentally sprayed her. That made her get a headache and we had to come home. Your mom said I should come over so Gram could get some rest."

Shermy kind of had a headache, too, from Shake's story. He went back to where he'd left off in his book. The main character was trying to start a fire without a match. Shermy didn't know how she was going to do that.

"I had to read that last year." Shake flopped onto the floor next to Shermy. "Want me to tell you how it ends?"

"NO!" said Shermy.

"What do you keep in that pouch?" Shake pointed to the treasure pouch hanging from a leather strap around Shermy's neck.

"Stuff." Shermy had to reread the page again.

"What kind of stuff?"

"Special stuff." Shermy shoved the pouch back under his T-shirt. "Shake, I am trying to read."

"Go ahead. I'll wait." Shake rolled Shermy's red-striped racer down the front of the dresser.

Shermy tried to keep reading. But Shake spun the wheels on the car. Too fast.

"Maybe your grandma is all rested now." Shermy grabbed the car and put it under his pillow.

"When she closes the door, that means 'Do not disturb.' Just like in a hotel," Shake said. "And she closed the door."

"Mom might want to make cookies. Why don't you see if she needs help?"

"She said I should see what you were up to." Shake picked up Shermy's T Rex.

"What about Brynn?" Shermy suggested.

"She's still crabby because I made origami frogs out of her coding camp homework."

"That was a whole week ago," Shermy said. "I bet she's forgotten."

"I bet she hasn't." Shake stomped T Rex along the bookshelf. A book fell off.

"Can you pick that up, please?" Shermy asked.

"Bad T Rex." Shake moved the dinosaur close to the book. "Oh no! His arms are too short." T Rex's arms flipped the book over and over. "He can't pick it up!" Shake waggled the dinosaur, making him roar.

Shermy felt like roaring, too. He squinched his eyes at Shake.

Shake put T Rex down and picked up the book. He shoved it back on the shelf.

"That's not where it goes," Shermy said.

"You sure are particular," Shake said. But he put the book back where it belonged. Then he flopped on the floor and swished his knees back and forth like windshield wipers. It was annoying. And noisy. But at least he was leaving Shermy's stuff alone.

Shermy found the place where he left off. It was an exciting part. Clio got the fire started, and Eli tried to catch a fish with a safety pin and the drawstring from his sweatshirt hood. The other kids in the story were off gathering pine boughs to make beds.

Shake tapped his feet. He wiggled.

Shermy turned a page. A bear had shown up in the

story! Clio screamed when she saw it. Shermy screamed, too. How would Clio get away?

"You're at the part with the bear, aren't you?" Shake leaned over his shoulder. "Don't worry. Eli throws a fish and the bear runs after it."

Shermy groaned. "I give up." He took a gum wrapper from his treasure pouch and slid it into the book to save his place. He wished he could tell Shake to go home. But he'd done that with Clair once when she'd come over to play, and Mom gave him a big lecture after. He had to make an "I'm sorry" card for Clair even though he really had wanted her to go home. He was stuck with Shake.

"Want to play space explorers?" Shake still hadn't let him have a turn with the helmet.

"Nah." Shake jumped up. "I feel like playing board games."

Shermy opened the game drawer.

"I have way more games than this at home," said Shake. "I have one whole closet just for games."

"These are the games I have," said Shermy. He didn't want to write another "I'm sorry" note. So he thought of another way to tell Shake to go home. "Maybe your grandma would let you watch a show?"

"I already used up my hour of TV today." Shake peeked in the drawer. "Hey! Pigs in a Poke! How about that?"

"That's my favorite," said Shermy.

They set up the game on the bedroom floor.

Shake grabbed the spinner. "Company first," he said.

"We usually spin to see who goes first," said Shermy.

"And I want to be the wolf," said Shake.

"Let's spin for it." Shermy always played with the wolf piece.

"I'm company," Shake repeated.

Shermy didn't think that someone who came over all the time could be called company. But Shake put the wolf on the start square. He spun the spinner. "A six! I get another spin!"

"That's not the way we play it." Shermy picked up the farmer and put it on the start square.

"Oh, I only got a two this time." Shake tapped the wolf across the board.

"You moved too many squares," Shermy said.

"Oops," said Shake. He moved the wolf back one space. "Guess I got carried away."

Sometimes kids miscounted and sometimes kids plain old cheated. Shermy squinted at Shake, trying to decide.

"Your turn," Shake said.

Shermy flicked the spinner.

"Look, you got a two, just like me!" said Shake. "I'm hungry."

Tap-tap. Shermy moved his farmer.

"My turn." Shake spun. "Another six." He moved the wolf. He twirled the spinner. "Aw, shoot. Only a four." *Tap-tap-tap-tap.* "Hey, now I'm way ahead of you."

"Only sixteen squares," Shermy pointed out.

Shake spun again.

"It's my turn." Shermy snatched the spinner away. "Five."

"Some graham crackers would taste good," said Shake. "Do you have any of the chocolate kind?"

Shermy ran his fingers over the wolf piece. "I'm pretty sure we only have regular."

"That's okay. I'll eat those," said Shake. "I'm kind of thirsty, too," he added. "Bring juice—I'm allergic to milk."

Shermy's teeth crunched together.

In the kitchen, Shermy poured two glasses of juice. "Whatever you command, your majesty," he muttered. He saw a brand-new box of chocolate graham crackers in the cupboard. He fished around until he found an opened box of the regular kind. He hoped they were stale.

Shermy carried the snacks back to his room without spilling one drop of juice. "Is it my turn yet?" he asked. He set the snacks down.

"Oh, I spun for you. You got a three," said Shake. He took one of the glasses of juice and—*glug-glug-glug*—drank every drop. "You landed on the return-to-start square."

"I didn't say you could take my turn." Shermy picked up his farmer and put it back where it had been. "I want to spin for myself." He did.

"Three!" said Shake.

Shermy counted. "One, two, three." He banged the game board as he counted.

"Hey, careful." Shake caught the wolf before it toppled over.

Shermy dropped the farmer on the start square.

Shake took his turn. He tapped his wolf along the game board. "Three-four-five." He clapped his hands. "I win!"

Shermy folded up the game board.

"Good idea," said Shake. "Let's play something else."

"Do you think you should call your grandma?" Shermy asked. "She might want you to come home."

"'Do not disturb,'" Shake reminded him. He pulled more boxes out of the game drawer.

They tried Snakes and Spiders, Worry, and even Jungle Journey. No matter what game they chose, Shake had different rules. And he always won.

"What time do you have to go home?" asked Shermy. How long were Mrs. Brown's naps, anyway?

"Oh, there's no rush." Shake rummaged around in the cupboard. "What else do you have?"

"Save and Spend?" Shermy suggested. That was another of his favorites.

"Boring." Shake flopped to the floor, making pretend snow angels and taking up all the space.

Shermy scooted out of the way of Shake's swishing feet. "I'm bored with board games," he said.

"Bored with board games?" asked Shake. "Me too!" He leaped up on Shermy's bed.

"No jumping!" said Shermy.

Shake boogied around on Shermy's bedspread. "I'm not jumping. I'm hopping."

"We're going to get in trouble!" Shermy only jumped on the bed when Mom was outside, busy with her painting or mowing the lawn.

Shake hopped higher.

"You're going to break my bed!" Shermy grabbed at Shake's arm.

"Missed me!" he teased.

"Boys!" Mom called upstairs. "Time for thirty minutes of fresh air."

"Good idea." Shake hopped off the bed. "We can play King of the Mountain."

Shermy got an idea. "I'll teach you how we play it here," he said. Then he smiled a very wolfy smile.

JULY

■■■■■■■■■■■■■

STAR-SPANGLED DAY

■■■■

"**D**id you remember the root beer?" Shermy asked. He was mashing egg yolks for deviled eggs. "And two kinds of potato chips?"

"And everything for s'mores?" Brynn tried on her new sunglasses.

"Check," said Mom. "And check again. Shermy, is your swimming gear packed?"

Shermy stopped mashing to give a thumbs-up. The Fourth of July was his favorite holiday. Fireworks, hot dogs, seashells, Frisbee on the beach, and, best of all, fireworks! "Check, check, check: swimsuit, towels, and my book, of course."

"I'll finish the eggs," said Mom. "Run over and see if Shake is ready."

"For what?" asked Shermy.

"I invited him to come along," said Mom. "His grandma needs a rest."

"Mo-om." Brynn took off her sunglasses. "Not two pesky boys."

Mom tagged Brynn with her *be nice* look. "It'll be fun. You'll see."

Shermy nibbled on a deviled egg as he went next door. Brynn always brought Kelsey. It was about time Shermy got to bring a friend. Well, bring Shake. He hadn't been so bad since Shermy beat him at King of the Mountain. Shermy smiled. Shake hadn't expected the water balloons. That was pretty fun.

Shake was sitting on his grandma's front porch. "Look what I'm bringing," he said. He had blue swim fins, a beach towel, and binoculars in his duffel.

"What are the binoculars for?" asked Shermy.

"To see the fireworks really good," said Shake.

"I'm going to get ours." Shermy ran home. Shake followed.

Mom and Dad were packing boxes in the kitchen. "That's a lot of stuff for one weekend," Shake said.

"Everything but the kitchen sink!" Dad laughed, then picked up one of the boxes. "I'm going to start loading the van."

"Can you get our binoculars?" Shermy asked. "I want to bring them along."

"Sure. I think I know where they are." Shermy and Shake followed Dad to the garage. "I thought they were right here," Dad said. "Hmm. Maybe they got moved?" He rummaged around on a shelf. "Eureka!" He handed the binoculars to Shermy, who put them in his duffel, just like Shake. "Now I better grab the rest of the boxes," Dad said. "We should've left an hour ago!"

Brynn and Kelsey came out of the house and headed for the van.

"Dibs on the back seat!" Shermy hollered.

Brynn made a face. "I already called it."

"It's my turn!" said Shermy.

Dad carried out the ice chest. "I think that's everything!" It took him two tries to close the van's hatch.

"Tell Brynn it's my turn for the back seat," Shermy said.

"Is not!"

"Is so!"

Dad held up his hands. "How about this? Kelsey and Brynn can have the back on the way to the cabin, and you boys can have it on the way home."

"That's okay with me," said Shake. "I like the middle row." He hopped in. On Shermy's favorite side.

"It's not fair," said Shermy. "Brynn always gets first dibs."

Mom started the van. "Here we go," she called.

Shermy buckled his seat belt. "I usually sit on that side," he said so Shake would know for the next time.

It was hard to be in a bad mood, though. Not with fireworks to look forward to!

On the way north, they played the Alphabet Game, Twenty Questions, and Car License Bingo. After the fifth game of I Spy, Shake said, "It's a long way to your cabin, isn't it?"

"Nearly to Canada," Shermy bragged.

"It's not too much longer," said Dad.

"The first one to spot the water gets a quarter," said Mom.

They played the Alphabet Game again. They were both looking out the window.

"Water!" Shermy and Shake yelled at the same time.

"Jinx!" called Brynn.

Shermy stuck his tongue out at her. Now they wouldn't be able to talk until someone said their names. Big sisters were the worst.

"Here are your quarters, boys." Dad handed the coins over the seat. Shake put his in his pocket. Shermy put his in his treasure pouch. He didn't say thank you because he couldn't.

"And here we are!" Mom eased the van down the long grass driveway to the cabin.

"Okay, Shake. Unjinx." Brynn pulled her overnight bag out of the van. "You too, Shermy."

"Race you to the beach!" Shake got ready to dash.

"Not so fast, fellas," said Dad. "First, we unload."

With everyone helping, the boxes of food and games and supplies were soon inside. "It seems like we're missing something," said Mom.

"This looks like quite a bit," said Dad.

"Where's the coffee?" asked Mom.

"It's got to be there," Shermy said. Mom could get grumpy without her morning coffee.

"Ta-da!" Dad held out a bag of coffee beans.

"That was a close one," Mom said.

Shermy rummaged in the other boxes. "Where are the fireworks?"

"I packed them in the old blue box," said Mom. "Then I set it by the kitchen door."

Shermy looked around. There were all kinds of boxes, but none of them were blue.

"Uh-oh." Dad pushed his glasses up on his nose. "Now I remember. I was ready to grab that blue box when I got distracted by looking for the binoculars."

"Not the fireworks!" said Shermy. "They're the best part!"

He and Shake went through everything. No fireworks. Not even one little sparkler. "Can we drive into town and get some?" asked Shake.

"I'm sorry, boys." Dad shook his head. "It's too far."

"But how can we have the Fourth of July without fireworks?" Shermy asked.

"There are lots of other fun things to do," said Dad. "Now, who wants to help me build the hot dog–roasting fire?"

"We will!" the girls pitched in.

"No fireworks?" said Shake.

Shermy's throat got tight. He shook his head.

"None at all?" Shake said.

"It's fun to collect driftwood for the fire," Mom said. "And don't forget these." She handed Shermy his glasses.

The boys gathered an armload of wood.

"This is not much fun," said Shake. "What about collecting shells?"

"I guess." That was usually Shermy's favorite thing. He knew the names of lots of different shells and rocks on the beach. Shake filled a bucket with plain old rocks, broken horse clam shells, and bits of driftwood. Shermy picked up only one shell. A purple mussel that he put in his pouch.

"Look at this!" Shake peered at Shermy through an amber-colored stone.

"That's an agate," said Shermy. "Those are hard to find."

"Cool," Shake said. He put it in his pocket.

"Yeah," Shermy agreed. "But not as cool as fireworks."

"Want to go swimming?" said Shake.

"Might as well," said Shermy.

While Mom watched, the boys jumped and splashed in the shallow salty water. Shake let Shermy try his flippers. And Shermy showed Shake how to poke at the seagrass to check for crab pincers.

After swimming, Shake taught Shermy how to make his favorite sandwich: peanut butter and sweet pickle. It was delicious. Later, Shermy taught Shake how to cook his hot dog with the perfect amount of black.

"This is great!" said Shake.

"Yeah," said Shermy. "But not as great as fireworks."

The boys waited for the cooking fire to burn down. When the embers burned orange, they roasted marshmallows for s'mores.

Shermy's marshmallow puffed up, golden and perfect. When he reached for the gooey treat, it fell off his roasting stick into the fire.

"These are good," mumbled Shake with his mouth full.

Shermy nodded. "But not as good as—"

"Don't say it." Shake poked another marshmallow on his roasting stick.

It was getting dark. The time when they would usually start the fireworks. "I'm done." Shermy's stomach hurt. And not just from too many s'mores.

"Me too. I'll be right back." Shake returned with his own binoculars around his neck and Shermy's in his hand. "Here," he said.

"What good are those?" Shermy asked.

"You never know," Shake said. "We might be able to see some fireworks from here."

They looked up the beach. They looked down the beach. They looked across the Salish Sea to the city of White Rock.

"Why don't they have fireworks over there?" asked Shake.

"Because that's Canada," said Shermy. "They don't celebrate the Fourth of July."

"Too bad." Shake flopped back in the grass, the binoculars at his eyes.

Shermy sighed. He was pretty sure you could have a Fourth of July without deviled eggs and two kinds of potato chips and s'mores. But without any fireworks—that was too much!

After a minute, Shake said, "Hey!"

"Hey, what?" said Shermy.

"There's a million, trillion, jillion of them!"

"Of what?" Shermy asked.

Shake pointed up. "Stars! I've never seen so many in my whole life."

"Stars." Shermy slapped at a mosquito. "You can see those every night."

Shake kept looking. "It's like someone spilled sugar all over the sky."

Shermy looked up, too. The stars did look like spilled sugar. He saw something else. "Hey, Falzar." Shermy pointed. "There's your home. Jupiter."

"Where?" Shake's binoculars waved back and forth.

Shermy helped him find the spot. "There."

"Jupiter." Shake said the word like he was casting a magic spell.

The boys were quiet, studying the star-crusted sky.

"This is cool." Shermy held the binoculars close. "Really cool, but—"

"Not as cool as fireworks." Shake finished Shermy's sentence.

They both laughed.

Shake hopped up. "I'm making another s'more."

"Okay," said Shermy. "I'm staying here."

And he did. For a long, long time.

BOOKS ARE BORING

■ ■ ■

Shermy set up everything just right under the tree. No wrinkles on the blanket. A bowl full of cheese crackers. A tall glass of lemonade with three ice cubes. A brand-new library book. He flopped down on his stomach and dived in.

"You're reading again?" Shake peeked over the fence. "Don't you want to play street hockey?"

"No." Shermy pushed his glasses up on his nose before turning the page. It made a loud crinkling noise.

He didn't usually make loud crinkling noises when he turned the page.

Shake climbed over the fence and flopped down next to Shermy. "So, what's this one about?"

"A story." Shermy took two crackers and kept reading.

Shake scooped up a handful of crackers. He crunched. Loud.

Shermy marked his place with his finger. "Shake, I. Am. Trying. To. Read."

"Do you want to go to the park?" Shake asked. "We could play space explorers."

Not even Shake's helmet could tempt Shermy away from his book. He finished another page.

Pretty soon, something tickled his ear. He brushed it away. *Tickle-tickle-tickle.*

Shermy looked up. Shake held a long piece of grass. He tried to tickle Shermy's ear with it again.

"Cut it out." Shermy batted the grass away. "Let me read."

Shake sat quietly for a few minutes. Shermy finished chapter one.

"This is boring," said Shake.

"Not for me," said Shermy.

Shake took off his flip-flops and stuck them on his ears. "Well, it is for me."

Shermy didn't look up from his book.

"Maybe I'll play street hockey by myself!" When Shake jumped up, he kicked over Shermy's lemonade, drenching the blanket and crackers. Shermy rescued the library book in the nick of time.

"Now look what you've done!" Shermy said.

"It's not my fault." Shake grabbed the book. "It happened because you always want to read, not play." He jumped over the fence, taking the book with him.

"You better give that back!" Shermy hollered.

"Shermy!" Mom called from the kitchen. "Time for lunch."

Shermy stomped inside. "I hope Shake goes home soon," he said.

"I know you don't mean that," said Mom.

"Yes, I do." He picked at his tuna fish sandwich. "All I want is a plain old summer. Like normal."

Mom set a glass of water next to his plate. She brushed his hair out of his face. "It's almost time to pick the girls up at the library. How about if I treat you to an ice cream cone on the way?"

Shermy doubted that even ice cream could make things better. But he didn't want to hurt Mom's feelings. "Okay." When they got back, he'd go get his book from Shake. Maybe take something of his while he was at it.

Mom let Shermy get a double-decker cone. He chose licorice and bubble gum.

"E-yew," said Mom. Hers was plain old strawberry. One scoop.

"Yu-um," said Shermy. He picked out the bits of bubble gum to wrap in a napkin. He put it in his treasure pouch to save for later.

When they got home, Shake was lounging on their front porch, drinking a carton of Jumpin' Juice and reading Shermy's book.

"You were right," Shake said.

Shermy stopped. "About what?"

"It's a good story," said Shake. "I'm up to where they capsize the canoe."

"That's where I left off!" Shermy said.

Shake ran his finger down the page. "You want to hear what happens next?"

Shermy covered his ears. "NO!"

Shake sighed. "Here you go." He handed the book

back to Shermy in slow motion. Then he trudged back to his grandma's house.

Shermy settled under the tree again. The blanket was still wet, so he just sat on the grass. He opened the book. The two kids in the story were in a tight spot. They managed to get to shore, but they had forgotten to pack a map. Imagine forgetting something that important!

Like forgetting fireworks on the Fourth of July.

Shermy looked over and saw Shake swinging, all by himself, on his grandma's big hammock. He was watching the clouds the way they'd watched the stars that night at the bay.

"Hey! Want to read this together?" Shermy called.

Shake scooted over on the hammock. "Come on over."

They got everything set up just right. Shake shared his Jumpin' Juice with Shermy. Shermy shared his bubble gum with Shake. Together, they shared the book right up to the very last, delicious word.

BERRY FUNNY

■■■■

"What smells so good?" Shake asked as they hiked along the creek in the park.

"Wild blackberries." Shermy pointed to the prickly vines growing alongside the trail. "Sometimes Dad makes pies with them."

"Pie?" Shake's eyes got big. "Pie is my favorite thing. Would he bake us one?"

"If we pick the berries, he would." Shermy sat down on a log at the side of the trail to shake a pebble from his shoe. Brynn and Kelsey, walking as fast as snails, finally caught up with them.

"Do you want to come back later to pick blackberries for a pie?" Shake asked.

"Yes to pie. No to picking," Brynn answered.

"Too prickly," said Kelsey.

"But Gram won't let me come to the park by myself," said Shake.

"Neither would Mom," added Shermy.

"There are a bunch of bushes in the vacant lot," Brynn said. "You could pick there."

Shake jumped in the air. "Let's ask as soon as we get home."

Mom and Mrs. Brown said yes. Dad found long-sleeved shirts for them to wear. Shermy rounded up two empty plastic buckets from the garage.

"How many berries do we need?" Shake asked.

Dad looked at their buckets. "If you fill both of those, I should be able to make two pies."

"Two pies," said Shake. "Let's get going."

Shermy and Shake crossed the street and walked down the block to the vacant lot.

"There are a million berries," Shake said. "Your dad could make a thousand pies."

"It takes a long time to fill one bucket." Shermy knew because he'd picked blackberries lots of times with Brynn.

"It won't take us long. We're super pickers!" Shake reached out to the nearest bush. "Ouch!"

"That's why Dad made us wear long-sleeved shirts. Because of all the prickers." Shermy nudged aside a long vine with his foot. He pulled off a couple of ripe berries. They smelled so good. Warm and sweet. But if he ate any, it would take longer to fill the bucket. He looked over at Shake. There was a purple stain around his mouth.

"Save the berries for the pie!" Shermy said.

"They're good just plain, too," said Shake.

Shermy weakened. He tried a couple. And a few more. But none were going in the bucket. "Okay. Here's the rule," he said. "You can have one berry after you pick fifty." Shermy started counting. The berries pinged into his bucket. "Forty-eight, forty-nine, fifty." He peered into the bucket. "Fifty isn't very many."

"And it takes two buckets for two pies." Shake sounded worried.

"Back to work," said Shermy.

"A bee!" Shake jumped back.

"That's just a honey bee," Shermy said. "It won't hurt you if you leave it alone."

"I am leaving it alone. But it's not leaving me alone." Shake waved his bucket at it. Berries flew out.

"Don't waste them!" Shermy picked the berries up and brushed them off. "Are you afraid of bees?" he asked.

"Of course not." Shake swished his bucket through the air again. More berries went flying.

Shake was sure acting like someone who was afraid of bees. Shermy laughed. Little old honey bees! Shermy started to tease him, but then he remembered that he didn't like it when Brynn bugged him about being afraid of cows. "Trade me places," he told Shake. "No bees here." Shermy moved out of the way and Shake hurried over.

The spot where Shake had been didn't have as many berries. Shermy squirmed around some prickers to a better patch. Then he spied an even better patch. But when he tried to go there, he couldn't move! An extra-thorny vine had snagged his shirtsleeve. "I'm trapped!"

"Super Shake will save you!" Shake put down his bucket and came to help. He tugged hard. "Oops."

Shermy looked at the hole. "That's okay. This is an old shirt," he said. "Is your bucket full?" he asked hopefully.

Shake showed him. "Let's put our berries in one bucket. To see how much we have all together."

Shermy poured his berries into Shake's bucket.

"Is that enough for one pie, at least?" Shake asked.

"No." Shermy was hot. And thirsty. "We need a whole bucket for a pie. Two buckets for two pies."

"Maybe one pie would be enough," said Shake. "How many pieces would that be?"

"Eight," said Shermy. "One for you, me, Dad, Mom, Brynn, and your grandma."

"With two pieces left over for the berry pickers!" Shake cheered. "Come on. With teamwork, we can fill this fast." He dropped some more berries into the bucket.

Shermy smacked his lips. Two pieces of pie! He picked a few more handfuls. But it was so hot. And he was thirsty. His arm stung from all the prickers. He ate a couple of berries to feel better. Picked a few berries. Ate a few berries.

After a while, Shake peered in the bucket. "Maybe we've got enough for a small pie?" He tried to sound hopeful.

Shermy wiped his sweaty face. "Not even a small one." He liked pie, but he was tired of picking berries.

Shake blew out his breath. "Is it enough for anything?"

Shermy thought. "Maybe a batch of blackberry muffins."

Shake gently shook the bucket. Blackberry perfume filled the air. "You know what my very favorite food is?" he asked.

Shermy was pretty sure he knew the answer. "Pie?"

"Muffins!" Shake lifted the bucket high. "Let's go home."

"Good idea." And Shermy ate another berry.

AUGUST

SHAKE UP

■■■■

Shermy was comfy on the couch with his new library book. He had a gum wrapper ready to save his place the minute Shake showed up. He read chapter one. No Shake.

He read chapter two. No Shake.

Shermy read three whole chapters in peace and quiet.

It was dreadful.

He put the book aside and walked over to the living

room window. He stared outside. Shake wasn't playing street hockey. He peeked out the back door. No Shake building forts in Mrs. Brown's backyard, either.

"Why are you pacing around?" Brynn asked. She was fresh out of the shower with a striped towel wrapped around her hair. She smelled like lemons and flowers. Shermy held his nose.

"I'b not bacing," he said.

She undid her towel and shook her wet hair like a dog.

"Watch it!" Shermy wiped smelly water drops from his face.

"Sorry." Brynn didn't sound very sorry. She went into her room and shut her door.

Mom was on the front porch, sketching. Shermy leaned against the arm of her chair. "That looks good," he told her.

"Why, thank you." She smudged a pencil line with her little finger. "What are you up to?" she asked.

Shermy sighed. "I was reading."

"Oh." Mom added a squiggle to the sketch. "Did you finish your book?"

."Not really." Shermy was pretty sure he'd forgotten how to read without getting interrupted by Shake.

"How about if we bake some cookies later?"

Shermy shrugged his shoulders so high they nearly touched his ears. He picked up one of Mom's paintbrushes and waved it around, making an air painting of a hockey stick. "Could Shake help?"

"Fine with me," Mom said.

Shermy perked up. "I think he's very good at measuring."

"Perfect," said Mom.

Mrs. Brown let Shermy in. "Summer is whizzing by, isn't it? It will be September before we know it."

Shermy shrugged. Mom had drawn a big red circle on the calendar for the first day of school. It still seemed pretty far away.

Shermy went down the hall to Shake's room. It used to be Mrs. Brown's rubber-stamping room. Shelves for

stamps and ink pads still lined the walls. But now they were holding all kinds of postcards.

Shake was reading one when Shermy walked in. Shake rubbed his eyes really fast before setting the post-card on a nearby shelf.

"Wow!" Shermy exclaimed. "That's a lot of post-cards." He started counting.

Shake sat on the bed and picked up a scruffy-looking stuffed owl.

"Thirty-nine!" said Shermy. "You could open a post-card store."

Shake waggled the owl's head in agreement. "Mom sends me a bunch every week."

"I've never gotten one postcard," Shermy said. "Ever."

"You can have them," Shake said.

"Really?" Shermy looked at him.

Shake waggled the owl's head no. "But I'd rather have my mom than any old postcard." He rubbed his face against the owl's used-to-be-white fur.

Shermy sat on the bed, too. The postcards were pretty awesome. Especially the one from Ireland. But he agreed with Shake. He'd rather have his mom and dad than postcards. Even of leprechauns. "Summer's almost over." He reached over and patted one of the owl's wings. "They'll be back before you know it."

"They've been gone eight whole weeks," Shake said. "Fifty-eight days."

"Fifty-eight!" Shermy exclaimed. Sometimes his

parents went away for a weekend and Grandpa Gordy would come stay. Even with Grandpa Gordy's famous chocolate chip pancakes for dinner, and movie nights, and Uno championships, those weekends seemed to last forever. Shake was so loud and fizzy. Shermy never stopped to think that he might miss his mom and step-father.

"We're baking cookies," Shermy said. He used a quiet voice like his teacher taught them so they wouldn't scare the class bunny. "Do you want to help?"

The owl's head waggled. Yes. "What kind?" Shake asked with a sniffle.

"I'm not sure. What kind do you want to bake?"

Shake thought for a minute. "Anything but oatmeal raisin. I hate raisins."

"Me too," Shermy fibbed. "Let's go."

Shake set the owl back on the bed. "I am a very good measurer," he said.

Shermy smiled. "That's just what I told Mom."

RHINOS IN THE GARDEN

■■■■

Shermy and Shake rested on the front lawn after a wild water balloon fight. Clair skipped up the sidewalk toward them.

"Come one, come all!" she called out. "Animal Fair at my house this afternoon at two o'clock."

"What are you talking about?" asked Shake.

Clair showed him a poster. "There will be prizes for the biggest animal, the friendliest animal, and the

most unusual animal." She hurried off down the street calling, "Animal Fair, Animal Fair!"

"I wish I had a pet to enter in the Animal Fair," Shermy said.

"Clair didn't say pets," said Shake. "She said animal. We can find an animal to bring. And win a prize."

Shermy rubbed his glasses on his T-shirt. "I don't know. Ryan's dog, Rufus, will win for the biggest. He comes up to here on me." Shermy drew a line at his shoulder.

"There are still two other prizes," said Shake.

"And Audrey's parakeet, Tigger, will win the prize for the friendliest. He talks to everybody," said Shermy.

"That leaves most unusual," said Shake. "Is there anyone in your neighborhood who could win that?"

Shermy thought. "I don't know. Most of the animals around here are dogs and cats and guinea pigs. Those aren't unusual."

"So we've got a chance!" said Shake. "Come on!"

"To the pond!" said Shermy. Off they raced.

They found frogs and tiny fish.

"E-yew. What's that?" asked Shake.

Shermy looked at the fat, slimy, yellowish creature covered in black spots. "Banana slug."

Shake wrinkled his nose. "*That* seems pretty unusual."

"Maybe in Walla Walla, but not around here," said Shermy.

"Too bad there isn't a prize for the slimiest," said Shake. "Where next?"

"We could try the vacant lot," said Shermy.

The boys poked around in the tall grass, avoiding the prickly blackberry bushes. Shermy picked up one bent Mr. Squish soda pop cap, a broken key chain, and a glittery pebble and put them in his treasure pouch.

"There are no unusual animals here," complained Shake. "Unless you count earwigs."

"Those aren't very unusual," admitted Shermy. This hunt was taking way too long. "We're running out of time."

"And I'm running out of ideas," said Shake. "Besides, I'm hungry. I can't think when I'm hungry."

"If we stop to eat, we will never find an unusual animal," Shermy pointed out.

Shake held his belly. "But I might starve!"

Shermy's own stomach rumbled. "A quick lunch," he said. "And we'll take it with us so we can keep hunting while we eat."

The boys made peanut butter and sweet pickle sandwiches and put them in a sack. Then they cut through Shermy's backyard for the shortcut to the park.

"Maybe we should look around here," said Shake through a mouthful of peanut butter. "You never know."

"I'd know if there was some unusual animal in my own yard," said Shermy. "Hurry up! The fair is about ready to start."

"What about that?" Shake pointed at a butterfly that had landed on one of Mom's pink roses.

The butterfly flicked its orange-and-black wings open and closed. Shermy hadn't seen this kind before. "That's very unusual." He bounced with excitement.

"I'll catch it!" Shake reached out. "Ouch!" He stuck his finger in his mouth. The butterfly flitted away.

"Watch out for thorns," said Shermy.

"Now you tell me." Shake shook his hand, but the thorn was stuck. He pulled it out and balanced it on his fingertip.

"Quit clowning around," said Shermy.

Shake picked another thorn off the rosebush and stuck it on Shermy's finger. "Now we're twins!"

"We don't have time—hey, wait a minute." Shermy peeled the thorn off his finger and licked its flat side before sticking it on his nose. "Look at me! I'm a rhino."

Shake stuck his thorn on his nose, too. "Now we are both rhinos."

"Snort! Snort!" Shermy pawed the grass.

"Snort! Snort!" Shake charged at Shermy. They tumbled to the ground, laughing.

"We've had deer and rabbits in our garden, but this is the first time we've ever had rhinos," Shermy said.

"It's pretty unusual," said Shake.

"Very unusual," said Shermy.

Everyone at the Animal Fair thought so, too.

FAREWELL, EARTHLING

■ ■ ■ ■

Shermy peeked out his living room window. A blue sports car pulled up in front of Mrs. Brown's house. A lady and a man got out and hugged Mrs. Brown.

Shake's mother and stepfather had come to take him home.

Now there'd be no one to bug him when he wanted to read.

No one to beat him at board games.

No one to hog all his crackers and juice.

"Boy, I'm sure glad Shake's finally going home," Shermy said. "Very, very glad."

Brynn looked up from making beaded friendship bracelets. "You don't sound very glad."

"You don't know everything." Shermy grabbed one of the beads and shoved it in his pocket. He ran outside. Take that, Brynn.

Shake's stepfather, Stan, was wrestling a suitcase into the trunk of the sports car. He took a smaller suitcase out. Put the big one in. Tried to put the little one back in. Took more suitcases out. It looked like he was working a jigsaw puzzle, only with suitcases. Stan's face was red and sweaty. He took something shiny from the trunk and set it on the ground. Falzar's helmet.

Shake stepped out onto his grandmother's porch. He carried a sleeping bag under one arm and a cowboy pillow under the other.

"Shake a leg, Shake." Shake's mother scooted past, carrying in-line skates and a hockey stick.

Stan closed the trunk with a grunt. "We'll have to put some of these things in the back seat." He put the hockey stick, the skates, and the space helmet in the car. Then he reached in his pocket.

"Picture time!" Stan pointed his phone at the boys. "Those are the longest faces I've ever seen. Can I get some smiles?"

He couldn't.

"I'll text this to your parents," he told Shermy.

"Thank you." Shermy remembered his manners. But he didn't care about a picture. It wouldn't be the same. There'd been many days this summer when Shermy had wished Shake would go home. But now that it was actually happening, all Shermy could think about was the fun: reading together in the hammock, the almost-fizzled Fourth of July, eating blackberry muffins, and even winning a prize at the Animal Fair.

Stan patted Shake's shoulder. "Just remember, you can see each other next summer."

"Next summer is a long way away!" Shermy and Shake said at the same time.

Shermy looked at Shake. Shake looked at Shermy.

"Jinx!" said Shermy. He smiled at Shake. Shake smiled back.

"Here." Shermy reached in his treasure pouch. He pulled out a gum wrapper, the mussel shell, and the Mr. Squish soda cap. "I guess I was collecting these for you."

Shake studied each item before putting it in his pocket. "Now I can start my own treasure pouch!"

"Come on, Shake, we've got to hit the road," called his mother.

"Just a sec." Shake grabbed the helmet from the back seat. He handed it to Shermy. "Farewell, Earthling."

Then Shake and his mother and stepfather drove off.

Shermy put on the helmet. It fit just fine. He went home and headed straight for the kitchen. "Hey, Mom," he said. "Did you know I have superpowers?"

"You do?" asked Mom.

"Yep." Shermy took a box out of the cupboard. "Just watch me make these Toaster Tarts disappear."

Dear Shermy,
This is your first postcard and it's from me! Cool! And guess what? We're moving! And you won't have to wait long to find out where.
Your friend,
Shake
Shermy Koda
522 Aster Lane
Bothell, WA 98011